LONG AND SHORT
SENTENCES

BAR NONE *Books*

LONG AND SHORT
SENTENCES

Rhapsody with BAR NONE *Books*

Rhapsody
61 Gainsborough Road, Felixstowe,
Suffolk IP11 7HS

ISBN 1 898030 12 X

Produced for BAR NONE *books,* Powys, Wales and
Arts Council England
WRITERS IN PRISON *network,* PO Box 71,
Welshpool, SY21 0WB

British Library Cataloguing in Publication Data
available.

Editor & Designer:
Clive Hopwood
and Sara Leipciger

Cover Illustration:
Hemera

This book was created after a series of workshops
by SARA LEIPCIGER at HMP Highpoint

Printed in Kent
by JRDigital Print Services Ltd
Rhapsody is the fiction imprint of Author Publishing Ltd

Contents

Godfrey's Number
Damien

"Hello?"

"Er, hi…"

"What can I do for you?"

"Em, eh, I… got your number from, em, the Blacksmith's Arms?" Tony's voice broke off in a nervous quiver.

"Oh – oh yes, I see," came a calm reply. "Do you want to meet up?"

"Em, I, I guess so."

"You don't sound sure."

"Well I've…" Tony responded quickly, then slowly added, "I've not really done this sort of thing before."

"That's okay. That's cool," came the calm voice. "First time for everyone. Let's meet up – you free now?"

"No!" Again, Tony's reply came faster than he would have liked. This isn't going well, he thought, it doesn't feel right… careful not to mess it up now. "Not right now, I'm busy. Maybe later? This evening?"

"Sure. Between seven and eight?"

"Yeah, yeah, that suits me fine." That's better. "Better make it eight. Where?"

"Do you know the Old Mill Pub?"

"On Victoria Street?" Tony asked, even though he knew exactly where it was. He'd walked past it plenty: a nondescript pub that issued no invitation.

"Out the back, there's a second toilet, in the yard – an old one; no one uses it." There was silence. "You still there mate?"

"Yeah. Yeah. Sorry mate," Tony said, "just writing this down." He wasn't writing anything down. I could still pull out… no pressure.

"So I'll see you there at eight?"

"Yes," said Tony, affirmatively. "Wait," he continued, "what shall I call you?"

"You can call me Godfrey. See you soon!"

Tony hung up. Godfrey... Godfrey! He wasn't expecting a Godfrey to answer the phone, but then he didn't really know what to expect. He sat for a while and thought about it. He thought about the voice, about how normal it sounded. He'd imagined he'd been talking to a rep from his credit card company. Yes Mr Sharpe, please do come in at your convenience. We'll fill in all these forms and your new repayment terms can commence straight away. Our new offices are in this dingy backyard toilet... Godfrey sounded so assured, confident. He was in control. Tony thought he sounded almost friendly and warm, like a friend, but Tony knew he would never be this man's friend. He couldn't help but try to imagine what the guy looked like. He couldn't get the image of a suit out of his head. The excitement began to grow in him again.

He gathered his thoughts and dialled the second number. It picked up straight away.

"Yeah?"

That startled Tony. He found himself repeating the same words as before, with the same hesitations. This time Tony suggested the meeting place, the Old Mill pub. His heart was pounding, and he felt uncomfortably warm. The air felt stuffy; his mouth was dry. The second voice was rough, more like what Tony was expecting. He had imagined the type of guy who writes his number on the wall of a toilet cubicle to be seedy – unsavoury. He had pictured a loner, a loser, a no-hoper. Someone who lives, then dies. Someone who doesn't affect the world. The kind of guy he could sit next to on the bus every day yet never notice.

Sometimes these types of guys came into the shop where Tony worked. They always went straight to the flashy new phones he knew they couldn't afford. They asked silly questions about ring tones and screen savers, not WAP capabilities and firewall connections.

They went to the covers stand to admire the shiny new bits of plastic and their shimmering colours. They never bought anything, five or ten pounds of credit maybe. Then they would shuffle out the door and back out into the shopping blur.

"What's your name?"

"Godfrey," replied Tony.

"Godfrey?"

"Yes."

"Okay Godfrey, see you at eight."

Tony felt relief. He sat in the silence for a while, thinking. A voice in his head was telling him to stop, but he ignored it. He got up and pulled the heavy curtains open; the shocking white light nearly blinded him. He opened the rickety sash window and the din of the coastal town gushed in.

That afternoon wore a hot and heavy cloak. Restless, Tony wandered about the town, hoping to kill some time. In fact, it worked oppositely. The minute hand pushed itself reluctantly around the face of Tony's watch. He watched people, men mostly. There were plenty more like him, wandering around the streets with no obvious agenda. He wondered what they were up to. Some turned out to be waiting in an agony of humid sweat for a partner to finish shopping. With others, he played a game. He tried to spot the shoplifter, the handbag thief, the drug dealer, the plain-clothes detective, next week's lottery winner and tomorrow's suicide. He wondered if he'd seen Godfrey already, or the man with the rough voice. He wondered where these two were now, and what they did for a living – who their friends were. He thought about following one home. An adrenaline-fuelled pulse rushed through his veins and swelled in his chest. What if he actually knew one of them? What if Mr Brandon downstairs was one? He liked the thought of that; he liked the idea of knowing someone's deepest, darkest secret. Maybe he'd follow Godfrey home, and to work, and one day orchestrate a

3

meeting, naturally. And he'd get to know him, befriend him, all the time knowing his little secret! He knew this wasn't healthy. But God, is life meant to be exciting, or boring?

Seven-thirty. Tony opened the door of the Old Mill pub. Every face turned with seeming anticipation. There was a hush. The bang of the door behind him signalled the resumption of a soft murmur. Tony ordered a neat whiskey, no ice, and downed it. He ordered another while he made for the toilet. He tried to make it look naturally, but knew he looked goofy, exaggerating a slight stoop to make it look like he was bursting. As if someone walks into a bar, drinks 250ml of whiskey and suddenly is desperate for a pee! Sod it, who cares? He figured these people had seen more suspicious faces than his own pass through.

Outside to the right was the toilet. It stood alone; old, crumbly red brick shedding from even crumblier plaster. It stank of old piss. The door was nobly three-quarter length and hung on loose hinges. It doesn't even have a lock for chrissake? Wet, mouldy toilet paper made an interesting model landscape of hills and lakes on the floor. Tony could hear a thousand stories cemented into these walls, but shut his ears. A shudder went down his spine. He looked at his watch. Ten minutes to eight. The cistern was high up, just below the ceiling. Carefully he stepped onto the toilet rim – there was no cover or seat – and padded the walls left and right with the tips of his fingers to keep his balance. He pulled both phones from his pocket and called one with the other. Immediately he answered one and wedged it into the recess above the cistern, lens facing out and down. Slowly he stepped down, careful not to splash. His stomach retched. He checked the screen of the phone in his hand – there he was. He felt sad. What am I doing? He paused. In front of him was a collage of old, faded graffiti. He scanned it for numbers, and found none. He sensed an urgency to leave, and returned to the bar. His whiskey was waiting. The plan was to stay there and see who came in, but all he could see were weatherworn faces with white bristles. He drank his whiskey and left. A short distance away was a remembrance garden. During the day it was busy with mothers and playful children. Later on it would be the social club of winos and tramps. Now it was empty, but for Tony and a phone. He sat and waited. The excitement had left him and was replaced with dread. He began to regret taking it this far.

He looked up, as if to heaven. The sky was now an even tone of pale grey. A seagull flew overhead, hovering for a while, its beady eyes searching the ground below. A gust carried it up and a flash of dying sunlight bounced off its wing. All was quiet. Tony looked to his phone and there was a man on the screen. Started, he looked around, making sure no one could see him. Tony felt uneasy. He took a closer look at the man in the toilet of the Old Mill pub. He looked smart, clean-shaven, and he was wearing a suit. Christ, it's Godfrey! Godfrey looked impatient; it was five past eight. He was fidgeting nervously in his pocket. Tony felt pleased with himself that his guesswork was right. He even felt empathy for the man on the tiny screen. And then a second man entered the cubicle. He was hard to make out… a baseball cap, dark clothing. They were discussing something. Tony held his breath; his heart stopped beating. The man in the cap moved first, dropping his trousers and facing the wall. Godfrey moved in close behind him, one hand on the guy's neck, the other on his trousers. Then Godfrey raised his arm, and pulled it down hard, and fast, again and again. Tony caught the flash of a steel blade. The man in the cap slumped to the floor. Godfrey disappeared, and Tony froze. His eyes welled up and he began to tremble.He felt very, very alone.He leaned back and looked up to the sky. He remembered the seagull, its beady eyes, and the flash of the golden sunlight on its wing.

5

Fidodido – A Boy in Love
Sherman

I knew this Fido when he was a boy of thirteen. He had a pleasant, ugly face, a laughing mouth and careless eye. He was about five foot two, short and slim, with a little patch of hair on the top of his head, shaved clean on the sides. He spent most of his time on the beach, thinking about love he was never going to find. With next to nothing on his brown body, he was as thin as a rail.But he was full of grace. He was in and out of the water all the time, scrambling up the sea-shells on his hard feet. His father was a fisherman who owned his own boat and sold his fish.

One day, Fido saw a young girl who lived in the town, and always bought fish from his father. Suddenly, Fido lost it, because of the girl. "My God," he said. "Am I having a dream, or is this real?" he kept looking at her, and licking his mouth, thinking of what to say to introduce himself. "Oh nonsense," he said, and stepped over to her.

"My name is Fido," he said. "Will you marry me?"

The girl was silent for a little while, and took a good look at him. She told him straight out, with the blunt directness of her race, that she could not marry a man who would never be strong enough to be a man. And, she said, her father would never give his consent.

Fido was terribly unhappy. But he did not blame the girl. He knew very well that a girl could not afford to marry a man who might not be able to support her. His smile was sad, and his eyes had the look of a dog that had been beaten, but he did not complain.

Unhappy Fido, his dreams of love still unwoken.

Making a Boob
XRIS

"No," she said in an even, measured tone. "I won't discuss it." The vinyl imitation walnut panelling absorbed the heat of her body just as he absorbed the heat of her words.

"Fair enough," he replied, as the sweat on his forehead ran, stinging his eyes. "I am off for a shower."

"I am doing it for me," she said defiantly.

"Darling, you don't want to discuss it, so there's no point in me trying to is there?" he asked reasonably.

(Have you ever noticed that if people have a strong opinion about something, being reasonable is like treading on a hornets' nest?)

"It's my body and I'll do what I want with it!" she shouted. "Don't walk away while I'm talking to you!"

"I love you and whatever you decide to do I will support you," he said.

"You are only saying that because you think I'll change my mind if I think you want me to do it!" she screamed at him.

"As you said, it's your body and you can do anything you want to with it," he tried. "Besides, I am too hot to argue. We've been in here for over an hour. I feel like I've sweated off a stone!"

(Arguing in a sauna is perhaps not a sensible thing to do, especially at 46 years old. It's a dangerous age anyway – no need to add to it.)

"You always look at other girls!" she shouted, almost crying now.

"I may look at them, but I live with and love you," he said tenderly.

7

She sobbed and hugged him, her body slapping against his, and buried her face into his chest. "They are small though," she said through tears.

"They are lovely," he replied.

"They sag," she bawled.

"So soft and silky," he said, caressing.

"I love you," she said.

"I love you," he said.

TV Paranoia
Samantha

They're talking about me again. Sometimes they do it in a good way, sometimes not, but they're still talking about me. And they're watching me, staring right at me, almost through me – I can't see why! There's nothing strange about me, but them? Well, they're an odd bunch.

The boy is called Jim. He's suntanned, a tad too much, with dyed blonde hair. He's not a real person: false hair, designer clothes to fit an image of what his friends want. He's not rude, nor polite, just anti this and anti that, the please and thank-you's are there, but with his feet on the chairs, belching and farting.

Then there's the big sister. Not bright, five foot nothing and just as wide. That sort of grey skin from lack of soap and water – add clothes to that lack of washing, and what a smell!

The parents sit on the couch, motionless, staring at me, intimidating me with their glare, as the children play out of control, abusing me as if I were nothing, had no feelings, no hope, no fire or passion. But I am unable to move, or resist them as they prod me, their fingers hurting me as they go – their toy. And I sit here and suffer at the hands of these intruders, my abusers, and say nothing. I'm motionless in terror and disgust, and at night I am left alone to recover from my hell.

Snapshot
XRIS

"What have you got there then?" he asked.

"Look!" Georgie said, handing him a photo.

A wave of mixed emotions and a half-forgotten past swept through him. The old black-and-white photo, turned brown with age, carried a whole set of luggage back into his mind.

"It's your great aunty. She married my brother about the same time I met your gran," he said.

"So she's my granty?" little Georgie said, sweetly with her little-girl lips through the gap where her two front baby teeth had been.

"I suppose she is; that's a nice word," he mused. His mind drifted back.

She'd been the idea girl. Beautiful, intelligent, popular, athletic. He didn't believe she'd even look at him, so he never made his feelings known. He distracted himself so as not to blurt out how he felt. But he had so much to say.

His brother had been terrible about girls, chasing and catching even the prettiest. There didn't seem to be anything special in what he said or did. It certainly couldn't have been his looks, or how he dressed. Girls just fell for him – and fell was the word. He didn't seem to care about their feelings at all. He'd just use them as a prop, as if to say, "Look what I have, look what I can do." He'd use them and discard them like the Sunday supplement.

That is, until Mathilde.

She was named after some old silent movie star, or a ballet dancer, he didn't know which.

At first he thought William (his brother, also known as Bill to his friends) was going to treat her just like he always treated girls, use her and throw her aside. It would have upset Georgie's grandfather badly if Bill had, and he would have sought some sort of revenge. Brothers know best how to cause pain. Georgie's grandfather fell for Mathilde.

At the time, he contemplated suicide, even bought rat poison.

Bill and Mathilde married, and Georgie's grandfather started drinking a bottle a day. A quart of JD numbed his pain.

The photo was taken before things went bad. Soon after they married, things changed.

Mathilde put on a lot of weight, became lazy, let the house and her appearance go. She became shrill and demanding, arguing and whining at him, making his life a misery.

And that wasn't all. She came on to every other man who appeared at the house. It didn't even stop there. Bill would find love bites on her body, and even found condoms around the house.

Finally, Bill had enough. They found him with his shotgun. He'd killed her, then used it on himself.

"Are you crying granddad?" asked Georgie.

"No sweetheart. It's just dust in my eye from all these old things."

The Crescent
Damien

I was a street urchin. At least that's what my dad called me. He wasn't amused when he said it. I spent most of my time in the lanes behind our house. I ate and slept in the house, and did everything else in the lanes. It's where I first kicked a ball, rode a bike, climbed a wall, threw a stone, kissed a girl, took a punch. I cut my knees on the curb and my teeth on the concrete. The lanes were the domain of me and our gang; it was our kingdom. Concrete and tarmac were my friends. I was comfortable with them, secure.

Then I found the scary place, The Crescent. It had been a very small private park once, with a grass tennis court – the kind English gentlemen played on before Independence embarrassed their serves. Now it was the thickest, fattest mass of briar and bush you've ever seen. Imagine a ball of wool, completely unravelled out of its ordered state into a tangled heap of wild strands. Now magnify that by fifty thousand and cover it in the sharpest thorns the size of sharks' teeth.

Pure evil. A tired, rusty railing with demon spikes protected it. Or maybe it was protecting us. Maybe that flaky iron was the only thing that stopped it from taking over the quiet, cosy terrace that tried to arch around it in a gentle embrace.

The gates weren't locked. There was no need for locks; nobody went in there. Except us. We found a small clearing that we could carefully pick our way through. Using sticks and steel bars – and other bits of detritus we regularly found around us – we beat back a path. It was hard work, and very slow going. But we took delight in beating the crap out of the bush. It was, after all, a living monster.

A dangerous one that bit back vivaciously if we weren't focused. It was the time of Feeling the Force, and oh, we felt it! And the monster felt the power of our light sabres!

There was an art to the fight. Confronted with a fat, woody, heavily barbed tentacle, if you didn't identify the weak point and strike it clean, it wouldn't break, but bounce back like an uncoiled spring; you had to be quick to duck. Scratches became a normality, an eaısily ignored hazard of war. It was when the thorns caught grip in your skin and refused to let go, and every slight move attracted another bite, that we paid for our endeavours with our blood.

The more ground we made, the higher the walls around us became. It got darker too, and a chill seeped out of the earth. Dead vegetation lay all around, the end of their struggle to escape the grasp of the evil enemy, starved of a gasp of fresh air, a sprinkling of sunlight.

It must have taken at least two weeks of hard battle before we reached a tree. It stood proud and firm, towering majestically above us. It cared nothing for us and our petty squabbles with the bush it dwarfed. But it made a good resting place, and the makings of an excellent den.

It really wasn't very long after that when the rumours began. No one knew who started them, but there seemed to be an uneasy amount of belief placed in them. They had to be true! Dracula's house was just over there!

A dilapidated house nestled in the middle of the terrace. It stood out from all the rest, with its dark, weather-stained exterior, overgrown garden and that cold look of an abandoned building. It was eerie. And we stood in the shadow of its walls. Now it all made sense. This so-called park was no park, but Dracula's garden! His cemetery even! This was no place to be after dark. Even on those hot summer days, an icy shiver would run down your neck, your skin would tingle with fear and you'd feel a primal instinct to run.

Soon all the trees had names. Whether one of the older boys christened them we never thought to ask – they seemed to fit so they must have been right! Our tree was The Tower. Three huge stumps powered out of one gigantic trunk and took the form of the towers of a Transylvanian castle. The tree called Eagle looked the creepiest – a massive tree, seemingly dead, with wide branches spread like an eagle preparing to take off. The Shapeshifter swayed and creaked and seemed to have a mind of its own. It was even said that you could see the face of Dracula in one tree if you looked hard enough! I never saw it, but I believed.

Although none of us dared to be afraid of The Crescent, the frequency of our visits declined throughout the summer. Maybe you can say we knew to respect the dark forces – I say we preferred the comfort of our concrete alleys.

At the end of the summer a film crew came along. It was so exciting that we all ran over as fast as we could. They wanted to film Dracula's house of course, and we wanted to catch a glimpse of the action! Only, something had changed since those first days of our war with the briared monster, and conquered our new territory. We'd grown up a little, and with that we'd become a little wiser. The truth came out, and we were ready to accept it. This was not Dracula's house after all. Count Dracula was in fact a fictionalised character in a novel, and this was simply the house of Bram Stoker.

Me and Rickey
Sherman

This story is based on me and a very good friend of mine. Twenty-four years ago, my sister took me to this little village called Charlemont in St Catherine, Jamaica, where we lived for some timeAt that time I wasn't attending school, but my sister was always working day in and day out. One morning, I woke up, looked through my bedroom window to catch some air, and was thinking to myself how good this was. I loved the beautiful morning atmosphere. Suddenly, I saw a boy looking straight at me, calling me quietly with one finger. I rushed out of my room and went over to see what the problem was, or if I could be of any help. When I went up to him I said, "Morning." He said, "My name is Rickey." I told him mine was Sherman, and from that moment on we became friends. In January, 1974, the journey of two best friends began. A journey that will last longer than both of us put together.

Did I say we were friends? Yessir. From that day, my eyes and his eyes made four. We began a journey which many people believed would end badly. But this was the best friendship anyone would want to have.

We were two of a kind. We had a lot in common; we did things no one would ever dream to do. Rickey was unique, and would do and say things that made others wonder.

Me and Rickey were like the seven days of the week, the twelve months of the year, the cartoons every kid wanted to see, the jokes that made you laugh, the film everyone was crazy about, and the bad chaos you didn't want to see (but you have to look, because there is nowhere else to look). Believe me when I say, we were hell and heaven together. Rickey's parents were the type of people who gave their child whatever he wanted. It didn't matter what. One day, Rickey's father said to him: "I am fed up with you."

"Why?" Rickey asked.

We thought there was something wrong; we weren't sure. "I'm goin' to give you access to everything, so you don't have to ask anymore," his father said. It was the best day of our lives. But two weeks later, Rickey's father was going away for a long time. He called Rickey to him.

"Do you know why I gave you access to the business and everything else?"

"No," Rickey replied.

"I went to the doctor and he told me I've got twelve days left to live."

We were terrified and sad, and we all began crying. I asked him where Mrs Bennett was, his wife. It turned out that she was making the best of the crying all by herself in the bedroom. Poor lady. I don't remember seeing her for about two weeks, and as for us, we didn't do anything crazy for about a year. This was a terrible tragedy, and happened upon us so suddenly, like an unexpected storm in the night. There was something about Rickey that always kept me wondering. He is about five foot two, short, brown and well built. And he never seemed to grow taller; I was about a foot taller than him. I once asked him how big he was when he was born.

"Why do you ask?" he said.

"Just wondering."

So he laughed and said, "Big enough!"

"You have to be more specific than that."

He paused for a moment, and laughed again, and after a few seconds he said, "Three feet."

"You're joking. So all these years, you only grew two feet." We both burst out laughing, and made fun of each other for the rest of the afternoon.

As kids, we often worried about getting old. However, many, like myself, were very curious about the adult world. Why? Because of the changes. In 1986, we both took huge steps towards the real world. The crazy world we had been in was coming to an end; it was now time for the real thing. Things like certainty, responsibility, sacrifice and commitment. This was a huge step for two young friends. Rickey was the type of guy who get nay deal or bargain with any company or factory. I was the one who saw that the bills were paid, and kept his father's business in line, all the time. If anyone needed to be hired or fired, I was the man to do so. Sometimes I didn't sleep for days. I was never happy. But whenever I go back in my memory through childhood, all my happiest memories begin with Rickey. If I should live my life all over again, I wouldn't change a thing. The only thing I would do would be to pray not to be an adult.

"You would?" Rickey once said to me.

"Oh yes, I would."

Rock Hotel
Dean

It was July, 1999. I was on the run, again, and I was in Newquay, Cornwall. This place is a bit like most seaside resorts, but the beaches are beautiful. The little harbour they have there just doesn't seem, in my eyes, to be in the right country. As pretty as it is, that's not my place. My place is a little further along the coast, about two and a half miles or so. I can't remember its name, but for me it is simply called Rock Hotel.

It's a little island, though only just. It has a little bridge as access. On this place, apparently, the chief used to live – maybe a thousand years ago. It's lovely to walk out over this little hill of pasture and then suddenly get a panoramic view of the coast, the ocean horizon and all that. There is a fresh sea breeze, insects, birds, the waves crashing on the rocks below: nature in its simple glory. As the sun sets, there's a great big jewel in the sky that kind of sprinkles millions of little diamonds across the floor of water in front of you. No wonder the chief had his hut out on the little island there. I was so captivated by this little place – it must have fallen from heaven – I decided to sleep right there on the rocks. Twice.

I Knew Her Well
Cecil

I don't have a lot of fond memories, but there is someone from my past I'll always remember. I think she was about fifty when she came into my life. She had a timeless beauty that kept her looking forty-something. Though her eyes were weathered and her hair was turning grey, and she had all the pains that accompanied a hard life, she was always full of life. I remember her cooking mostly. Her recipes seemed made up, like a witch's brew: a pinch of this, the eyes of that. But when you tasted her food, you were hooked. She was always singing, or talking in some strange language to herself. People thought she was a witch, and would sometimes go to her for potions. I'd see her handing them little bottles with instructions: "Rub this in before sleep," or, "bathe with this twice a week." Sometimes when she got mad, she'd curse me out with your mother this, or your mother that.

Which is funny, because, she is my mother.

A Life on the Run
Dean

Around about '96 or '97 my friend Matthew and I were on the run from the police, for various things really. We were basically on an adventure. It was madness: scary, funny and enjoyable every mile. We had decided to try and find a way to hitchhike to my hometown, and see what we could do in order to stay away from the Essex police. I must say, I was more excited about the prospect of going up north than Matthew!

Anyway, we bunked the train to Norwich and slept there overnight, and then set out for the North the next day. We got quite a few lifts surprisingly, considering the fact that we were two teenagers – I mean, most people wouldn't stop for one. Eventually, we reached my hometown and ended up sleeping in the haystacks of a farm I knew to be just down the road from where I lived with my Nan before she died. It was great to be in the fresh country air, just the same as I remembered it to be.

We went to the town centre the next night and while we sat on a bench in front of the harbour, wondering what to do with ourselves, this old guy came and plonked himself right in between us. I thought it was a bit cheeky, but what the heck; he was this harmless old boy. Then he started talking – I don't know why. Maybe he could sense we were bored or something. The first thing he said was that he used to have his own boat. I looked at him and thought "used to" sounds about right. He was dressed like Paddington Bear: yellow rain hat and matching jacket. He looked a bit alarming.

"Now I'm a vagabond," he said.

I was confused now. "What's a vagabond then?"

He proceeded to tell us that basically it's just someone who just goes around doing this or that, without actually doing anything. At least that's what I thought he meant.

"So what happened to your boat then mate?" Matt asked; he was becoming curious too.

"The Navy got it."

"Hey?" Matt and I looked at each other, and then at this guy. He was just staring straight ahead, looking into the past as if it were rolling through the harbour right in front of us. This guy needed a shave. He was funny looking too, but I put it down to the lighting. He took his hat off, ran his nicotine-stained fingers through his hair, and took a cigarette packet out of his breast pocket and offered us both one, which we accepted. He gave us both a light, lit his own, and took a big drag.

"Well," he said, as a big plume of smoke exited his mouth and nose into the now-fading light, "they didn't actually get it as such, they just kind of sank it for me. Right in front of where we're sitting."

Matt and I must have both looked across the harbour because the old boy laughed and said, "It ain't there now though."

I was hooked. "So why did they do that then?"

"Well, they'd been chasing me for over 20 years, all over Europe. They caught up with me here – well my boat anyway – and they sank it, just like that."

"Did they ever catch you?"

"Nope. Though, sometimes I wish they had really!"

Neither of us bothered asking why he felt that way. I can't speak for Matt, but I myself, young as I was, knew what he meant. Life spent running away may be a form of freedom, but you're never really free at all. Your life has more limits to it than it did before.

"Seven different countries. That's how many places I've tried to settle in," the old boy said. "And in more than one town too. Not really a city-goer myself – too many people to cause problems, and also I couldn't really stray too far from S.W.E.E.T.S."

"Who's that then mate?"

"Who's Sweets? That was me boat. It stands for: Someday, We'll Even Enjoy These Stars. Seems like I was always chasing them on the horizon. One day I remember thinking to myself, you can't run for eternity. I was actually saying it to the stars, and somehow I felt the stars were saying it back to me. Me and Sweets ran together for a long time. We went all over Europe. Couldn't stay anywhere for too long, 'cos the Navy kept catching up to us. I always slipped through the net though. I guess that's why they chased so hard, like the big fish you try to catch. I was their mission."

"Well, if you don't mind me asking mate, why were they chasing you?" I asked.

"Ah well, believe it or not, I didn't do anything. To start with. It was either May or June, 1965 I think... funnily enough, it was right here where it all started. Well just there, look, around the corner."

Matt and I both got up and walked to the railings so that we could see a bit further down the harbour road.

"You see it? The Jolly Sailors."

It was a nice looking pub, black beams and little circles in the glass panes.

"I was in there, watching these really pretty women dancing and chatting up the fellas. I had my eye on this one girl, pretty as the springtime she was. When I saw her on her own, I went to talk to her. I hadn't even managed to get both my legs out from under the table when I lost my balance and knocked into this fella and caused him to spill his beer. I tried to apologise but this bloke was having none of it. I was suddenly surrounded by sailors."

"What happened next mate?" asked Matt. "Did you have a tear up?"

"What, a fight? No way! I pushed through them and got out of there, as quick and graceful as a cat on a

22

hot tin roof. Never been one for trouble, me. Luckily, old Sweets was tied up right here, so I made straight for her and got my nut down."

I looked out the harbour, trying to picture it. The old boy took out his cigarettes and offered us each another one, which we accepted, all the while staring out at the invisible past in front of him.

"As I emerged from below deck in the morning, I looked up and was as shocked as he was to find us staring at each other. It's quite evident, today especially, that this guy was the type to hold a grudge.

He was leaning on those railings there, probably just trying to sober up enough to go back to his own ship. As soon as I saw him, I recognised him as the guy from the pub, and he, I don't know how, recognised me. Probably from the look on my face. My instincts told me to get out of there. Silly, really, when you think about it. simply could have just apologised for the night before and then played it by ear. Before I knew it, I was in the engine room, starting the motor. As I ran up to untie the lines, this guy was coming down the ladder to board me. I just panicked, and went to the cabin and threw the throttle forward, full speed. The guy was screaming blue murder at me as the lines snapped as he was trying to climb aboard. He missed, and fell in the harbour. That's how it started."

"What, the chase?" I asked.

"Yes, my friend. Life on the run."

I have to admit, I chuckled to myself when he said that. If he only knew! "So what happened then? Where did you go?"

"Well, everything I needed was on Sweets, so I sailed down to Southampton, stayed there for a few days, then went on to France and down the Costa del Sol. I never really stayed anywhere for too long, and after about sixteen months or so, I wound up in Italy. My first port of call was a lovely little town called St Raphael. At least, it looked lovely anyway, what I saw of it. When I was about fifty metres from the harbour, I noticed a little outboard full of sailors coming towards me. I thought nothing of it at first, but then one of the sailors was standing and shouting as it drew near. I thought it was a case of mistaken identity so I let them almost come aside me. Then I recognised the one doing all the shouting. He must have seen me click because he said something and they all started shouting. I slammed the speed to full throttle and yanked the wheel to port as hard as I could and ended up clipping their stern just hard enough to topple the sailor out the boat. It was as I came level with the coast that I noticed a Navy frigate, the HMS Star, anchored just off shore, about eight hundred metres out to sea. Funny how you don't notice things until it's too late. Sweets was fast, but not that fast. Luckily for me, they didn't see what I'd just done to their shipmates – at least I think they didn't because they didn't give chase. I sailed straight for Corsica, cursing my luck all the way. For about three months, I went around the whole island, stopping here or there, but my money and supplies were low and there wasn't much to be made by a lonely Englishman.

I decided to hit mainland Italy again. I went to Roma for a few months, but there wasn't much to be made there so I headed further down the coast to Napoli. I managed to get a job there, hiring out my boat for transport. Occasionally I'd be taking people to places, mainly Sardinia, otherwise it was just crates. I'm sure half the time I was shipping illegal contraband, but I never looked and never really cared. I needed the income. Then one day I was taking one guy on his own to a little island called Isola di Pantellaria, in-between Sicily and Tunisia. It was a good trip really, and the guy, Luca, paid me well. It said he could bring more work my way if I wanted it, so I took up his offer. I ended up doing runs to Malta, Sicily, back to Pantellaria and then onto Tunisia and occasionally Sardinia. Sometimes people, sometimes boxes. Mainly boxes though. I was well paid. I did these runs for about four years and never gave any thought to the Navy in all that time. I was saving money; I had girlfriends all over the place, a villa here, a room there. Life was great. Then I was asked to take a shipment to Venice. It was quite a simple trek, and I would be paid well, so I agreed.

I did wonder, at this point, why they were using me and my little boat when they could just as easily fly their shipments and pay a lot less. What the heck though. None of my business – or so I thought. I stopped off in a place called Malfetta, and as I went into the harbour master's office I nearly had a heart attack. On the notice board there was a picture of me on my boat (named Monica at the time) with "wanted" written underneath it. They didn't give my name, but you could tell it was me and my boat. I was wanted for more than I stood to read. Attempted murder of eight British Royal Navy sailors, drug smuggling, gun running, importation of illegal immigrants – the works. They all wanted me: Britain, France, Italy. I shot out of that harbour quicker than you can blink."

"So what about the delivery to Venice?" I asked as I looked across at Matt. He looked like he was struggling with the suspense that I had unwittingly laid on the tale.

"Well, I set out for the deeper parts of the Adriatic Sea and then checked what was in the cargo. My world was now bad, but as soon as I opened that first crate it got worse than bad. Take my advice lads, don't be ignorant in your business with things..."

"Yeah, yeah," Matt said, cutting him off. "What was in the crates?"

'Well, the first one I opened had what appeared to be little ceramic houses. Then I smashed one by accident trying to open another crate. There was a bag of powder inside it. There were ten crates with the same contents, brown powder. Then I started opening up other crates and found guns inside them. I couldn't believe how stupid I had been. Bloody ignorant fool more to the point. Then I dropped another crate and ended up with blocks of some type of putty all over the floor. I didn't know what it

25

was at first, then I remembered hearing about this stuff that the military used, plastic explosives. To think I'd just dropped the stuff, never mind transported it all over Italy. It took me four and a half hours, but I dumped every last crate over the side of the boat and got the hell out of there. I was pretty panic-stricken, because not only did I have half a continent looking for me, I would now probably have the goddamn Mafia after me, too. I didn't know what else to do so I just headed down to Greece and prayed I wasn't wanted there as well. I hit a little island called Paxo, just down from Corfu. That's where I had Monica repainted and named Sweets.

I hung around Greece for about three years or so, here and there; I even tried to settle down a few times, but that's a different story to tell. I kept getting spooked by one thing or another. Then I went to Turkey for a couple of years. Nice place Turkey, but not my cup of tea. I just didn't feel comfortable, and everywhere I went, I heard stories about the Navy this, the Navy that. I'd had enough. I decided to come back to old Blighty. Problem was, I had to run the gauntlet through the Mediterranean again. I got as far as Sardinia before I ran into any problems. I was having engine trouble, and not for the first time mind. She served me well, but I was quite demanding at times so I couldn't blame her for starting to fall apart on me."

He breathed a deep sigh as he must have wondered how bothered his engine had become. I looked at him and could almost see the pain etched in his face. He didn't look so rough to me anymore, or alarming. He actually looked like a kind and gentle sort of bloke, but also formidable as well.

"So, I stopped at a place called Carloforte on the Isola San Pietro. I couldn't get the parts I needed there, so I caught a lift to the mainland and had to go across the island to the city of Cagliari. I got the parts I needed, which were small enough for me to fit in a back pack, and I set off back to Sweets. Just outside the city, someone recognised me and all hell broke loose. People were screaming, whistles blew, sirens started getting louder and louder, but then it just went dark. I came to, to the sound of gunshots and people yelling. There was a stand-off between three guys, Mafia perhaps, and about twenty police. I remember being dragged, and then thrown into a corner in some dank and smelly room. These three guys were screaming at each other and waving their guns around, popping the odd shot out a window every now and then. It seemed like hours. Suddenly, the room erupted with pandemonium. There was crashing, gunshots, bullets ripping through the walls, windows coming in. The place had just been stormed. It was a joint enterprise between the Sardinian police, the British Navy and the nasty-looking Italian Naval Squad. For all that effort to capture me alive, or at least save my life, those buggers nearly scared me to death. Anyway, they slung me in an ambulance and checked me over, then threw me in a car. I even still had my backpack with me. And who goes in and sits next to me?"

Matt said what I was thinking, "The sailor!"

"Ya. Had to happen sooner or later I s'pose. Ten years or so he'd been trying. I told him I was getting parts for my boat and was just on my way back to Pasada – a little fib – to repair it when that all happened. But then all hell broke loose again. Gunshots and bullets were pinging everywhere. The driver started the car and floored it. He drove so badly, we crashed on the second bend. We were all knocked for six but I got my wits about me before they did, and managed to grab my bag and scramble out the broken window. I ran like hell. Anyway, although I wanted to do just what my instincts suggested and hide in a hole somewhere, I managed to eventually get back to my boat. It took me a painful day and a half, I reckon. It took me forty minutes to do a repair job that should have taken a few hours, and then I was gone.

"No messing about lads; I only stopped three times on my way back to old Blighty. I stayed in Southampton for two years but I was always paranoid there. Then I gradually worked my way back up here and settled down for about eight years until one day I came out the Jolly Sailors and saw the HMS Star sitting in front of my sinking Sweets. If they could find my Sweets, with a different colour and name, I knew they would be able to find me.

"I've been a vagabond since. It's an adventure, an easy life, but it's not really freedom, is it? A life on the run!"

As he said this to us, he got up. He kind of did a little stretch, turned to face us, gave us his packet of cigarettes and said, "Think about that before you lads run any further eh?"

I watched the old guy as he nonchalantly strolled on his way when Matt dropped the packet of cigarettes. I looked down at him as he was picking them up and said, "Matt, did you catch his name?"

"No, I never heard it mate."

We both flicked our heads to shout after him, but he was gone as suddenly as he'd arrived.

"Life on the run hey? Whew!"

"What shall we do then?

"Dunno."

"So where should we go?"

"Dunno."

Home
XRIS

The iron gate is made of curls of wrought iron. It squeaks as you trip the latch. It grinds as if in pain when pushed open. Coming down the concrete path, there's a bit of a flowery smell from the chrysanthemums and roses on either side. Stepping up onto the tilted alcove, with its brick arch and chest-high columns, cupped with bevelled shrubs, there is the front door (you were maybe expecting a portcullis and a drawbridge?).

Shove in the Yale key and push the door open to the hallway, floored with wood planks. The walls are covered in floral-print paper, the kind with gold flecks in it.

There's a mirror to your right (which can be kind of scary at night if you're on drugs!) and shelves over the heater. This is to the left, at the bottom of the stairs.

Up the stairs, and turn right at the landing and continue up the stairs, then turn right towards the front of the house. It's the second door to the left, and it looks like a bomb hit it. Yes, it's my room.

Climb in, and over, the clothes and shoes, books and random other things on the floor (ah, I remember what I wanted that for... but I digress). For those people who cannot abide clutter and mess, perhaps we should move on (I am not a sadist!).

Coming back the way we have come, to the stairs, down to the hallway and into the front room, there's a settee in front of the telly (or a couch in front of the tv for our transatlantic readers) where I spend most of my waking hours in the house.

We Were Used to It
Damien

Our house in Ireland was usually cold. Not that I really noticed, or cared. My room was my sanctuary, my place to hide, my space to be free. My fingers always seemed numb, still functioning yet anaesthetised. There was an old iron fireplace that was never lit. Maybe we couldn't afford the extra fuel, maybe the chimney was blocked – I just knew not to ask. Occasionally I had the use of a gas heater, but it made my eyes sticky and my head tired. The cold didn't really bother me then, not like it does now.

The ceilings were all high in the house I grew up in. One time, one of them fell down! My parents were out, and we were just old enough to be left alone, my sisters and me. We had just left the room, having pushed to the limit our bedtime. Then, crash! The carpet was white with dust and crumbly plaster. I wondered who would be cleaning that up?

There were always lorries parked on our road. Big, fat, hunky steel trucks. One of the neighbours owned them, and ran his business from our street. These were the days before Europe dragged us into civilisation, and anybody could do anything they liked, wherever they liked to do it.

Our house used to shake. The old wooden sash windows would rattle and a new hairline crack would appear somewhere. It was something we were used to, the deep-throated rumble.

It was always a noisy house. Everyone shouted. My parents at each other, my sisters at me. Me at my sisters. The trucks added to this, and so did the kids on the street, and the planes overhead.

The planes overhead. Sometimes they scared the shit out of me. I could picture them almost scraping their underbellies on our roof. The nightmares began when I saw the front page of our national rag-mag, and its story of what would happen to Dublin if a Hiroshima-type bomb landed on the General Post Office. I used to wake in the middle of the night to the sound of piercing jet engines, and look out the window, and wait for the blinding flash.

Master Black
Cecil

I grew up near my primary school in Trinidad. It was Roman Catholic, and had a small church on its grounds, which everyone from the neighbourhood would go to. There was an L-shaped canal, about four feet deep, that ran behind the church and to the left of my schoolyard, which had been paved so it could act as a parking lot for Sunday mass. There were no fences around the river ravine, as we called it, because it acted like a moat, defending the church and school from the small forest-like growth and bush that had reclaimed the land beyond, where the trains used to run. During the dry season, there was little water in the moat. Enough dry points were exposed so that you could hop over the water and climb back over to the other side. Most kids would stay on the school side and try to catch the small freshwater fish that swam there. These fish would leap out of your net, and if you threw them on the banks, they would try and make their way back into the water. We liked to catch these long, black eels, even though we were told that they would turn into zombies and bite our little toes off. We liked to parade them around, to see who had the best tail, and at the end of the day, we would throw them back in. Not because of the old wives' tales, but because there was only one fish worth keeping: Blacko Jr, son of Master Black. Now, Master Black was the king of all ravine fish. He had a three-inch body and a four-inch tail that would open up like a Chinese fan, which extended out with long blue, orange and yellow streamers that darted in the air every time he leapt out of the water. No one had ever caught him.

One day though, he was spotted hiding under a rock upstream, just where the river went underground. All the fishermen lined the banks. As soon as someone lifted the rock, Master Black shot out like a bullet. It was sheer pandemonium. Kids were falling in; water was flying everywhere. In the end, he nearly evaded us all. But then, probably as he turned around to laugh at us, some kid saw him and threw a rock. That was the end of Master Black. His son became a legend as well. He wasn't as big, but just as elusive. I gave him the name Blacko Jr, but I found no joy in hunting him and I lost interest in the ravine.

The Ford and Firkin
Dr Punk

One night a few years ago, my friend Warren and I decided to go out for a few beers in a pub called the Ford and Firkin. Now, the Firkin wasn't a bad boozer, I mean, it played rock, was open 'til twelve, and served these horrifically strong real ales, so off we went. On the bus, Warren rolled a couple of joints while I forced a few pills down my neck, washed down with Tennants Super. These pills weren't all that strong, I thought, but they were okay with the beer. I grabbed a few and swallowed them with the sickly sweet taste of super strength lager.

Warren gave me a bit of a funny look and suggested I slow down a bit.

"Nah… I'll be alright." I took one of his joints and started toking happily. Warren sparked up too, and it wasn't soon before the bus driver came up and told us to get off before he called the law.

By the time we got to the Firkin, it was nine and the place was heaving. The pills were really catching up on me, and fancied just sitting down and having another beer. I spotted a table in the corner with two birds sitting by themselves. I fancied a challenge, so I gave Warren a nudge and we bowled over there with our pints. He tried to say hello, with difficulty over the noise of Motorhead doing Ace of Spades, so he stood there like a lemon grinning insanely, and propping me up.

One of them said something, which I hoped was "sit down", so we did. Warren was still smiling and not saying much, so I thought I better say something before they told us to piss off. Thing is, my eyesight was going a bit funny too, and these lovely young ladies were now in tunnel vision. They were nice though. Slim, young, just the right blend of tattoos, piercings and hairdye. I'm sure they were smiling back at us.

Before I knew it, they were leaning over us, yelling over the music, and the conversation was on. It turns out that the lovey I was talking to was Mel, and Warren's minx was Sandra – or something. But it was getting bloody hot in there, and I was slurring badly. Mel was not impressed. She hadn't told me to f—k off yet, but I was waiting for it.

Warren was doing all right though. He and Thingy were so closenow; they were almost touching and there was loads of eye contact and smiles.

I decided to give Mel another go, and although I was speaking slowly and trying not to dribble on her, it was pretty obvious she'd given up on me.

Bollocks then, I thought, and made my way to the bar, which was surrounded four deep. I drunkly pushed my way through and eventually caught the eye of the tired old peroxided barmaid Jackie. I ordered a pint and shot and put my money on the bar, and wondered for a moment why Jackie was able to understand me when Mel couldn't.

Back at the table, Warren asked the birds if they wanted to come out and smoke a blunt with us. The girls eyes lit up at the prospect of free drugs, and eagerly followed us out back, like two rats following the Pied Piper. Mel seemed particularly keen, and was quick to get out there.

Warren built a monster, this thing was massive. He stuck it in his gob and lit it. It smelled pretty good too, and the flash bastard knew it as he inhaled deeply and passed it to Thingy. She took a couple of small puffs, then passed it to Mel. Mel took it and smoked like a pro – holding the smoke down, and letting it back out again, slowly and gently.

She smiled at me and passed what was left of Warren's monster over. I wasn't in the mood for it, but smoked anyway, and watched in disgust as Warren and

Thingy started kissing and feeling each other up. Great. I wondered whether or not to bother making small talk with Mel, when she beat me to it.

"Look, I'm sorry about in the pub just now. I couldn't really hear you over the music, and you sounded pretty drunk. I don't want you to think I'm a bitch or something."

Well, this came as a bit of a shock to me, and I didn't really know what to say, when suddenly she started kissing me.

Now, this ain't bad, I was thinking. It's been a while, and it's getting late...So I kissed her back. But the evening was starting to repeat on me, and I was feeling a bit unwell. I pulled up for air, but she held my face and kissed me again, exploring my mouth with her tongue. It was too much for me, I tried to pull away, but she held me like a vice.

I could feel it rising in the back of my throat, and then, I did it. I threw up. All over Mel. She was in hysterics, punching, scratching, biting, crying, calling me every bastard she could think of. But I was so ill, I didn't care. Stomach cramps seized me. I was bent double, with Mel still hitting me, and then I fell to the floor.

I could hear Warren laughing, and feel Mel kicking. My eyes were closing.

Then, Warren had a hold of me. He was still laughing, and dragging me off to the night bus, and telling me how I'd ruined his lucky chance with Thingy and what a w--ker I was. We didn't go out drinking as much after that.

The Hidden Truth
Mark

Most people who come to England from Jamaica are in search for a better life. That is why some take very dangerous chances, like carrying drugs to the country. I know the public may look at these people as criminals, but they wouldn't understand why these people are determined to take the chance, to leave Jamaica. Poverty and safety are the main reasons for leaving, but there are other things as well. For instance, some people don't even have a toilet bowl or pit, so they have to go deep in the bush or wait with a lot of strain until night time so that no one can see them. But this is just the tip of the iceberg. Right now, many Jamaicans have a better life in English prisons than they do, living on road, at home.

People tend to choose England because of our understanding of the country, which is one of the wealthiest in the world. Our forbearers already slaved for England, we are mixed in relations, the English still make our currency, and some people even consider England as a mother country.

I managed to escape the suffering and was accepted in England, but only as a visitor with no permission to work. Ninety-five percent of the Jamaicans who come here, come as visitors because there is no other option. After being here a while, and being convinced of the luxury of living here and by my mother's support, I decided to stay and make myself a better person. My first aim was to further my education so I started to attend college while my passport was surrendered to the Home Office.

After my college fee was paid, I had to attend four days a week. It was getting too hard for my mother, because she was the one who was buying the food, our clothing, and paying the rent. I wasn't the only one; I have four sisters depending on her also. At that time, I was desperate to do some work, even though I wasn't allowed to. But this was the prime time of my life, so I sought, and was refused by a lot of places until I found a cash-in-hand job as a construction worker. But this wasn't too reliable, because it was on-again, off-again and sometimes it took a while for work to resume after it had stopped. This went on until the person who hired me retired. He recommended me to someone else, but after three weeks, this person asked for a National Insurance number, which I couldn't produce. So I lost that job and this National Insurance number turned out to be my biggest problem. Everywhere I applied, they turned me down because I didn't have one.

I came to the understanding that I could work 20 hours a week, but had to go through the college to get my number and a bank account. But the college said that I had to get my passport back from the Home Office before I could apply for anything. I was confused. It wouldn't help to ask the Home Office for my passport, because I didn't want to disrupt the process of them extending my stay, and it wouldn't make sense, if they weren't going to extend my stay, to apply for a number. So I just left it at that point.

Things got worse when my girlfriend got pregnant. She is also Jamaican, but doesn't have any other family, like I do, to help her in this country. We had to live together at my mum's with my four sisters and my mum's husband. It caused some problems because the place wasn't big enough. I heard about a place where we could squat for a while. I also stopped going to college to try and save as much money as possible so we could rent a decent place when my girlfriend had the baby. We were not entitled to a council flat, which would have been cheaper. When it was coming closer to her time to give birth, we rented a room for seventy-five pounds a week. To pay that much money, we never knew where the next payment was coming from, which added to the stress of having a baby on the way. We managed until she was born on January 3, 2003, a lovely baby girl. I started back at college after a while, because my mother fell in love with the baby and helped a lot to support us while I tried to get a qualification at the college.

This went on for a while until the baby started to demand more things.

We received a booklet for the baby about benefits. We had to fill in some questions, but one of the first questions asked for either of the parent's National Insurance numbers. So we had to ignore the booklet because we didn't have numbers. And we didn't want the Home Office to refuse our request for an extension on our stay because we showed a dependency on the government.

My friends helped, but then they introduced me to drugs so I could help myself. I thought about it a lot before I decided to try it. But my friends stopped helping me, and then I experienced the worst period of my life, watching my baby's last tin of feed finish. That's when I made up my mind to try selling drugs. I was aware that it was a crime and what would happen if I got caught, but I couldn't bear watching my baby go hungry. We almost got evicted by the landlord so I had to take a chance. And I ended up in prison.

Most Jamaicans face the same problems, and that's why so many are in prison today. When we come into this country, the benefits that would make life easier don't apply.

I know I did some things wrong, but I feel I am a victim of the system. But I am willing to survive my four-year sentence. If the government made it easier for people to get National Insurance numbers, many Jamaicans wouldn't end up in prison, especially the ones who are willing to work. Instead of using undercover officers to support and then arrest us, they should do something that would help some of us solve our problems.

I understand that the amount of prisoners has doubled over recent years. I think this is partly because after we serve our sentences, and try to restore ourselves back in the community, we are the least likely to get hired because we are still serving sentences with that criminal record on our backs. How can we survive without committing more crimes? We might have to do more, and end up in prison again. The prison population will always be increasing.

Live Gig
Dr Punk

The best part of going to see my favourite bands live (apart from getting my head smashed in the mosh pit!) has got to be the dry ice. You stand there with your mates in the venue, drinking expensive gnat's-piss beer, enduring the second-rate support acts, while you wait for your heroes backstage to put their drugs down, pick their instruments up, and get their arses on stage. Suddenly it happens.

The amateurs on stage leave, and the venue is plunged into darkness. Interval music creeps out over the speaker system and the dry ice belches onto the stage. Your heroes walk on, and a deafening roar of delight resonates through your ring holes as thousands cheer their approval.

You faintly hear the 1, 2, 3, 4 count over the crowd, and then it kicks off – big time. Everyone is headbanging, pogoing, crowd surfing, moshing – call it what you like, it's hectic. Blood spills from broken noses and split mouths, punches are thrown – it's chaos.

We've all paid fifteen pounds to be deafened, ripped off with crap beer, and have the shit kicked out of us by our fellow gig-goers.

This is hardcore, and I love it! Next week is a punk all-dayer – wanna come?

Near Perfect Balance
Anon

The frozen caps of the planet. Earth's water storage system at either extremity of the globe. The fluid planet, the perpetual cycle of water, circulating until it reaches the extreme latitudes that encompass the outer polar caps, where it freezes as ice. It is freezes into slabs the size of continents, into frozen floating mountains. Nature's water system: the near perfect balance. The often-heard scenario of the ice caps is that they're melting, and that the earth's landmass can flood and be submerged beneath the melting ice. The North Pole has no rock or solid ground, only that of frozen water. A massive area that touches Russia on one side and Alaska on the other.

I.C.E.
Dean

It's frozen water, cold and hard. If dropped, it shatters into shards. Clean or dirty, black or white, always dangerous when it's night. Not a problem in the day, for any kids who want to play. Everyone likes it in their drinks; I like the sound it makes, kurplink! Something pure but something fake, something simple but something great.

Jack and the Bookcase
Damien

Old Mrs Crow was having problems with the key. Jack gave her a hand. A bit of jiggling and a solid shoulder got the door open. Only Jack entered. The first thing he noticed was the chill in the air. It soaked through him, clothes skin and bone, like an icy-cold liquid. He stepped forward. The floorboards moaned in pain under his feet. Around him, Jack saw an assortment of shapes covered in dusty calico. Straight in front of him was a large Gothic window, with a few small panes missing, the remainder encased in a crusted frost.

Shafts of blue-white moonlight illuminated a bookcase in the corner of an otherwise dark and foreboding room. Jack shivered. He made for the bookcase slowly, as if he had a limited amount of time to survive the frozen atmosphere. The book he was after jumped out at him. He pulled one hand from under an armpit and reached for it. It almost hurt to touch. It wouldn't budge. Jack tried to tighten his grip but his fingers felt numb. As he squeezed, tiny darts of pain shot up his arm.

He pulled at the book; it groaned but wouldn't move.

"Are you all right, dear?" called Mrs Crow from the dimly lit doorway. "I'll just go down and put the kettle on."

Jack pulled his other hand out. With the old lady gone, he could give it a good go. Both hands clasped the spine of the fat old book. Using his knees for leverage, he pulled with all his might. The book groaned more and the cabinet began to rock. Jack was breathing hard; his breath formed beautiful fractal clouds of exhaled air. One last, mighty tug. The bookcase shook and tilted forward. Jack tried to let go, but his fingers were stuck hard to his prize. An almighty crash, a cloud of dust, and Jack was no more.

Street Ice
XRIS

"It's a menace and I want it off the street," the lieutenant said at roll call. The precinct was tasked daily, usually with pretty ordinary stuff, car crime, burglary, etc. It was because a twelve-year-old girl had died from it. So, off went the black-and-whites, with the shotguns on the dashboard, and riot gear in the trunk. Off to cruise the main drag and roust a few low-lifers.

And Jonesy went to college. The argument had taken about an hour, her partner was all SOP (and being an SOB). Finally he saw sense. A designer drug needs a designer. Let everyone else look for the retailers, she was after the research and development department. The forensic lab had provided them with a list of what was in this crap, and it was mainly organics. The first port of call was the technical college, because it was known for its Organic Chemistry courses. Several MIT graduates had started here. Katherine Jonesy and her partner arrived and asked to see the doctor in charge. Central casting at New Line Cinema would have hired this guy to play Dr Frankenstein.

"What we are after is a list of people capable of doing this, people who might have a reason to do so," Jonesy told the doctor.

"I really can't think of anyone who would think of doing something like this," he said. "I teach all my students to do science for its own sake. Not to make money."

After prompting and some clever questions from her partner (his strength) about mood swings, absences, debts, arguments and cheating, they had a list of people to see. Katherine's partner complained about the amount of work she was creating, (and calling her Katherine, not Kat, was designed as a petty act of revenge). She knew he was going to grumble about this for weeks.

The first job now was to go back and update addresses for these suspects. Back at the precinct house, they were called in to the lieutenant's office.

"What are you doing?" he asked.

Kat explained her thoughts, and waited for the explosion. It didn't come; he said, "Interesting approach, go with it."

Top of the list was Henry Simpson. He lived with his mother and was always in debt. He had two jobs when he was in college to try and keep solvent. As a result, he missed a few lectures and did pretty badly in his final exam. They called at his trailer, and spoke with his mother, one of those perpetually invalid women who complain about everything and dominate anyone they can. (Think of Norman Bates' mother in *Psycho*). She hadn't seen him for several days; all she could tell them was that he seemed to have a lot more money than she'd ever seen him with before.

Kat knew they could not be that lucky, that the first person they checked on was their perpetrator. It could possibly have happened one time in a million that the chief suspect was on the top of a list. They had to follow it up, even though it was so unlikely. Going to the address she'd given them, they asked the neighbour. The guy said that Henry was working as a pharmacist assistant in a drug store on 5th Avenue.

Sure enough, there was Henry in the back room mixing up prescriptions to a set of instructions left for him. A few questions later, he was put far, far down the list. So the search went on. Frank Hopkin had been arrested for hash. But it was probably not going to be him either.

His work address was on the database because he had an arrest record. It was a chemical supply house, and he was the supervisor, his certificate qualifying him to deal with the poisons register.

"So, Frank, tell us what you know about Ice," Kat's partner said.

"We don't carry any, this place doesn't even have a fridge," he said.

It was pretty obvious he had no idea what or why they were asking, so they left him to it.

The radio blared to life calling for assistance. There was an officer down, and a gunfight going on. Kat and her partner raced to the scene.

A Girl I Once Rescue
Sherman

After chatting and drinking with my friends in a pub one night, I was walking home along the road. Suddenly I came across a few lads and a girl a few yards ahead of them. The girl was walking very fast and looking behind her every second, crying, so I began to hurry to catch the girl. As the breeze goes by I smell tobacco and alcohol as if the lads were carrying the pub with them. After catching up the girl and asking if I can be of any help she said, "Yes."

I said, "How?"

She explained the situation to me, so we both began to talk.

I asked if she knew them. Either she don't hear me or she choose not to answer.

We walked on in silence.

Some yards on I sensed we were still being followed. I turned round and saw them coming.

"Please let's carry on. Ignore them," she said.

"Is that your boyfriend?" one called out. He was clearly drunk.

I felt the tension in her body as she moved closer to me.

"I'll get you," the lad called out again, "you'll be mine I'll get you."

"My journey is over," I said. "Will you be O.K. now?"

"No," she replied.

"Where are you going?" I asked.

She said Sunny Hill but she need a cab. So I called the station and give my address.

Desperately I wanted to sleep and it occur to me to invite her in until the cab arrived. I couldn't leave her outside alone because she was obviously in some kind of trouble. My conscience wouldn't allow me to sleep. I told her I had to rest but she could wait in my room. Here, under the light I saw her properly. She was slim, almost skinny, her loose fitting cotton dress, far from concealing, accentuated her bony hips.

I offered her a drink which she accepted. She sat into the armchair drinking her drink.

"You didn't answer my question," I said.

"What question?"

The drink seemed to have revived her. I detected a note of aggression in her voice.

"Did you know them?"

"Does it matter?"

"If I save someone from drowning I would be curious how he or she fell into the water, whether, maybe, he or she did it deliberately."

"Sorry," she said in what was almost a whisper. "Those guys have been troubling my life for weeks. Every night they wait for me."

"You owe them something?"

"No," she said firmly.

Suddenly she sat upright. "I went with one of them one night. They were violent, very violent. I did not want to go with them tonight so they threaten to rape me. That's why I ask you to help me."

The cab arrived. She stand up, adjusted her dress and perfunctorily brushed her hand in her hair.

"Thank you very much," she said.

"That's all right," I said with more nonchalance than I intended to.

Untitled
Dr Punk

When your flame burns low
And cold winds moan
Harsh winter ever-near.
When your light grows dim
Your struggle within
Is more painful every day.
Searching fruitless for the sunlight
But can't get beyond the ice
Playing on your own persona.
Questioning your life
Living life in shadows
In an empty ravaged shell.
I long to see gardens
But lay chained down in hell.
Oh paradise, I long for thee
To walk amongst thy trees
To gaze upon thy beauty
A gentle summer's breeze.
I long for new beginnings
With constant prayer for change
But I'm still denied my sunlight
Burdened with these chains.

Love
Samantha

Visions of princess and Angels
A sweet dream of the most beautiful woman,
The more pleasure, the worst pain,
Dreading the end of my tomorrows,
Dreaming of some forever.

The amber star that stole my heart,
The princess star that holds the key,
Is there a chance that there's a moment,
Holding hands and running free?

How long would it be before I told her,
The emotion I feel that flows through me,
The pain in my heart when she was leaving,
Dreaming of some forever.

The amber star that stays in my heart,
The princess star that holds the key,
Is there a chance that there's a moment,
Holding on forever.

Visions of knights and ladies,
Days of heroes and heroines,
And their love forever and ever,
Valiant deeds of daring, passion and woe,
Walking on water and floating like snow,
Dreaming of some kind of forever.

Life's Worth
Cecil

Joy wouldn't feel so good, if it weren't for pain.
Sunshine always feels best, just after the rain.
You can't miss what you never had,
but you can long for it all the same.

Man,
If you live on the ocean,
You can't fear getting wet.
In other words,
life wouldn't be worth a damn,
if it weren't for death.

Root of all Evil
Sherman

Facts, philosophy
the love of money is the
root of all evil;

It seem to be for some people;
misers love their own money
and thieves love other peoples!
Money.

Money causes many people to lie, rob, murder, thieve,
          and betray their friends,
but money itself is surely not evil;
it is nothing more than a necessary part of our everday
lives.
So why does it often appear
as a motive of crime?
Are greed, envy, needs and poverty the causes?
Do thieves see the means of it that other people can't
see?
Don't ask me.

A Giving Taker
Dean

With contempt I lay the strands along the centre of its life
and gently form a particle of death.
It's almost like commitment to a hated, needed wife,
just to keep the peace and give it breath.
I've tried so many times to get divorced from this disease,
but every time, I've tried to no avail,
I no longer take advantage of the produce from the trees
(O^2)
and everything I eat could well be stale.
It leaves me out of pocket, out of breath and in despair,
It hate it yet can't stand to be departed.
Every time I light one, I am forcing you to share,
forever I'll regret the day I started.

Bad Day
Cecil

It's 6am and I got a hangover.
I should get out of bed, but it's so hard to roll over.
Can't call in sick, the boss won't hear it.
I'm going to miss the bus, man I just know it.
So I'm late! Don't throw a fit!
Sorry Mr Cornwall, my car in on the fritz!
Man, I need some coffee, but not on my shirt!
I want to say, you stupid bitch!
But instead it's, sorry, are you hurt?
I got to leave, I can't believe, it's only 10:30.
I know there's a God, and I'm sure he hates me.
Oops, here comes the boss, got to look busy.
Jackson, come here for a minute.
Go f--k yourself!
Yes Mr Beasley?
Your work here is really good.
Oh no, here it comes.
But I regret to inform you.
Knew I should have brought my gun.
It's due to company cutbacks.
I'll give you a cutback.
 We have to let you go.
I understand, I'll clear my desk.
You can finish the day.
No thanks, I'm going home, and get some rest.

Ups and Downs
Sherman

When things aren't going
quite well,
as you would like them to,
and with the dawn
of each new day, your skies are less than blue,
remember
I believe in you
and I know you have inside the strength you need
to help restore your
confidence and
Pride!

Untitled
Dean

Awake in my sleep, and so slow though I'm fast,
I fall to my knees and I weep,
I ponder the choices I've made in the past,
As I sow the moments I reap.
So often the reaping has set my heart weeping,
So often the sowing is slow.
Fitfully sleeping while strange dreams are speaking,
of a long life that shortens in growth.

A Shadow of a Doubt
Dean

Some things I am sure of, yet I still feel uncertain,
it's like I find this window, and then someone draws the curtain.
Hearing someone speak is one thing; what they say is another,
can you understand what's written, if you only see the cover?

At times we can be so sure that we feel we want to shout,
but then our voice is smothered with a shadow of a doubt.
Did that really happen? Are you sure that's what he said?
Suddenly a thousand questions roam around your head.

Out of faith comes certainty, out of hope comes doubt,
tomorrow may not come, so now's the time to find it out.
When you want an answer, you must ask a question first,
you have to drink life's water, if you want to quench life's thirst.

Don't let doubt defeat you; keep defeat at bay,
use it as an instrument to help you find your way.
Often doubt will creep up, challenging your sense,
like when the serpent asked of Eve, "Is that really what God meant?"

Unsure of where we come from, we're unsure of where we'll go,
doubt becomes a shadow in the light of what we know.
Because of all the shadows cropping up, here, left and right,
we need someone to guide us who can keep us in the light.

The day you ask for Jesus is the day your life will change,
shadows start to wither as you call upon His name.

About the authors

Sherman is 31 years old and was born in Jamaica.

XRIS is 46 years old, or 7, 252 (and counting) days, depending on how you count. He says: sayin' what I say is sayin' what I see.

Simon is the product of an urban council estate.

Cecil was born in Trinidad.

Damien is 33 years old, and a London-based film production designer.

Samantha is 46 years old, and more than the average woman.

Dean currently of HMP Highpoint. He is learning to live a good life and waiting to do good things for God.

Dr Punk would like to say: screw you, and everything you stand for.

Mark was born in Jamaica in 1977. He writes about the hidden truth, and is a very straight and factual person.

Also from BAR NONE *Books*

THE TIGER BENEATH

Writing from
HMP Brixton,
HMP Holloway
& HMP Wandsworth

"Thoughts and ideas
long imprisoned"
Prose and poetry from
three London prisons
ISBN 1-874600-87-2
£2.99 80 pages A5

THE WIND THAT STIRS

Writing from
HMP Manchester,
HMP Preston,
HMP Styal &
HMP Low Newton

"It is important that we
believe in ourselves and
in our dreams"
Prose and poetry from
four Northern prisons
ISBN 1-874600-88-0
£1.99 48 pages A5

THE TALKING ROCK

Writing from
HMP Long Lartin,
HMYOI Glen Parva
& HMYOI Swinfen Hall

"You can hear that in your
silence, and tomorrow
build your new self"
Prose and poetry from
three Midlands prisons
ISBN 1-874600-89-9
£1.99 48 pages A5

Author Publishing Ltd
61 Gainsborough Road Felixstowe Suffolk IP11 7HS

Specialist book producers
trying to help writers reach readers.

Book publishers with over 40 titles in print under the
Rhapsody (for fiction) and Braiswick (for non-fiction)
imprints we also assist authors and independent
publishers to bring work to print .

We also run

www.author.co.uk

The UK site for writers and independent publishers

Links to useful contacts for writers
Ezines full of information
Authors own pages